My "a" Sound Box®

WRITTEN BY JANE BELK MONCURE • ILLUSTRATED BY REBECCA THORNBURGH

The Child's World®
childsworld.com

Published by The Child's World®
1980 Lookout Drive • Mankato, MN 56003-1705
800-599-READ • www.childsworld.com

ISBN HARDCOVER: 9781503823044
ISBN PAPERBACK: 9781503831261
LCCN: 2017960280

Printed in the United States of America
PA02430

A NOTE TO PARENTS AND EDUCATORS:

Magic moon machines and five fat frogs are just a few of the fun things you can share with children by reading books with them. Reading aloud helps children in so many ways! It introduces them to new words, motivates them to develop their own reading skills, and expands their attention span and listening abilities. So it's important to find time each day to share a book or two . . . or three!

As you read with young children, you can help develop their understanding of how print works by talking about the parts of the book—the cover, the title, the illustrations, and the words that tell the story. As you read, use your finger to point to each word, modeling a gentle sweep from left to right.

Simple word games help develop important prereading skills, including an understanding of rhyme and alliteration (when words share the same beginning sound, such as "six" and "sand"). Try playing with words from a book you've just shared: "What other words start with the same sound as moon?" "Cat and hat, do those words rhyme?" The possibilities are endless—and so are the rewards!

My "a" Sound Box®

This book concentrates on the short "a" sound in the story line. Words beginning with the long "a" sound are included at the end of the book.

Little  had a box. "I will find things that begin with my **a** sound," he said.

"I will put them into my sound box."

Little  put on his hat and went for a walk.

He found apples, apples, apples.

Did he put the apples into his box? He did.

Little 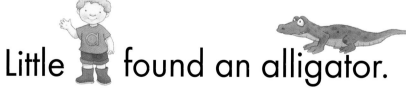 found an alligator.

Did he put the alligator into the box with the apples? He did.

Little  found ants, ants, ants.

Did he put the ants into the box with
the apples and the alligator? He did.

Little  found arrows, arrows, arrows.

Guess where he put the arrows?

Next, Little  found an ax.

It was a toy ax.

Guess where he put the ax?

Now the box was full. It was so full . . .

. . . the ants, the arrows, and the ax fell out.

The apples and the alligator fell out, too.

"Now who will help me fill my box?" said Little .

Just then, an astronaut came by.

"I will help you," said the astronaut.

We will fill your box.

Guess what happened next?

The astronaut took Little  for a ride.

Up, up, and away!

Little 's Word List

alligator

arrow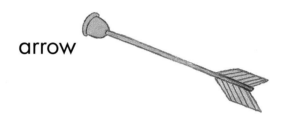

ant

astronaut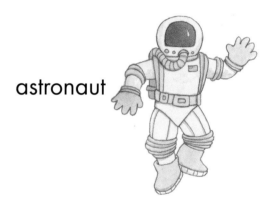

apple

ax

Other Words with the Short **a** Sound

acrobat

anchor

arm

ambulance

antlers

armadillo

Words with the Long **a** Sound

Little "a" has another sound in some words. He says his name, "a." Can you read these words? Listen for Little "a's" name.

acorn

ape

apron

angel

April

More to Do!

Little  met alligators and ants in this book. But there are many more **a** animals! There are aardvarks, albatrosses, anteaters, and armadillos. Maybe some of these are your favorite animals.

You can make an accordion book about your favorite animals—no matter which letter they start with. Ask an adult to help you.

What you need:

- heavy white paper (4 inches by 18 inches)
- 2 index cards (4 inches by 6 inches)
- scraps of wrapping paper
- stickers for decorating
- markers
- glue

Directions:

1. Fold the paper in half.

2. Fold each side in equal parts so the book looks like an accordion.

3. Glue one index card on each end to form the book covers.

4. Decorate the book covers with scraps of wrapping paper and stickers.

5. Use the inside pages to draw animals for your book.

6. Ask an adult to help you write a sentence about each animal under its picture.

About the Author

Best-selling author Jane Belk Moncure (1926–2013) wrote more than 300 books throughout her teaching and writing career. After earning a master's degree in early childhood education from Columbia University, she became one of the pioneers in that field. In 1956, she helped form the Virginia Association for Early Childhood Education, which established the first statewide standards for teachers of young children.

Inspired by her work in the classroom, Mrs. Moncure's books became standards in primary education, and her name was recognized across the country. Her success was reflected not only in her books' popularity with parents, children, and educators, but also by numerous awards, including the 1984 C. S. Lewis Gold Medal Award.

About the Illustrator

Rebecca Thornburgh lives in a pleasantly spooky old house in Philadelphia. If she's not at her drawing table, she's reading—or singing with her band, called Reckless Amateurs. Rebecca has one husband, two daughters, and two silly dogs.